Supreme Joy

Foreword

Murli Chari's latest aphoristic book 'Supreme joy' is to be 'chewed and digested' (Francis Bacon's phrase from his essay 'Of Studies') as it requires thorough, critical examination and reflection. The book has an unputdownable quality to it. The essence of his nous and profound thinking is obvious in this book which's a compendium of choicest aphorisms and their excellent explanations. Chari is a bibliophile who reads and loves to cogitate. He believes in Rene Descartes' dictum, 'Cogito, ergo sum' (I think, therefore I'm). He's a seasoned writer who has penned many books. Writing is not his profession. It's his passion. Years of voracious reading enriched his cerebral persona, expanded his horizons and deepened his perceptions. So, whatever he writes, reflects the depth of his mind and breadth of his vision. He doesn't believe in lush wordiness. His writings are bereft of linguistic gymnastics because he refrains from flaunting his command of

Supreme Joy

English. This creative honesty makes him different from run-of-the-mill writers whose sole (and also 'soul') objective is to show the power of their quills. Murli Chari wields a formidable pen but remains away and aloof from the limelight. His whole life and creativity vindicate the famous quote that a genius thrives in a state of solitude. That doesn't make him a recluse or a misanthrope. Chari loves to interact with people but at the same time, he also loves the quiet moments of introspection. Believing in the Shakespearean wisdom that 'Brevity is the soul of wit,' Murli Chari writes in a precise and succinct manner. That's why he loves aphorisms. All the aphorisms in 'Supreme Joy' are Chari's intellectual regurgitations. Being an original writer, he creates his own gems. All these aphorisms are his own creations. This slim book has 56 chapters and there're headings and subheadings in every chapter for the convenience of readers. All his books are

Supreme Joy

very reader-friendly. For example, the heading of chapter 19 is, Relax, everything is fine. The subheading, A relaxed mind conquers all, amplifies it. Then he explains the aphorism in his inimitable and engaging manner. The readers feel intellectually rejuvenated and empowered. When Chari says, 'No laws are sacrosanct' (Chapter 9), he means it. He's a rebel and a radical who swims against the tide and calls a spade a spade, nay, a shovel. Read this gem of a book and feel intellectually uplifted. May more such pearls ensue from his pen. We need more and more writers like him because they help us succeed and evolve. To encapsulate, Chari's latest book must adorn your bookshelf.

Sumit Paul, A Poona-based independent research scholar who reads, reviews and dissects books

1

<u>Happiness itself is enough for a great life.</u>

Any pursuit other than happiness is a chimera -   Murli Chari

All human endeavors are directed towards happiness. The very purpose of life is happiness. All the living beings are happy but it is only human beings driven by greed for more and more invite misery. Hoarding and hankering after material riches lead us to strive and create stress. Contentment and joy within make us feel bliss. Gautam Buddha said so beautifully "We are self-sufficient. We need not seek external things for happiness." Happiness is a state of mind. When we become ambitious, we cross many people's paths. All the crimes and war are anti-happiness. Crimes are committed for material gains which may not ensure happiness. Though we are affluent we are miserable. Being rich does not guarantee happiness. Happiness does not cost us

Supreme Joy

a dime. Watching tides on an ocean for hours together provides happiness in immense measure. Watching the children play and observing their innocent smile give us humongous happiness. All animals except human beings are always happy. Our dogs are so happy that they give us unconditional love and are very playful. Being with friends and resorting to banters provide happiness in great measure. Even those who lead hand to mouth existence are happy. On the other hand, even, the filthy rich are miserable. It's a colossal waste of time, money and energy to garner more and more whereas happiness does not require much. Greed is leading us astray. Simple things in life provide immense happiness. True happiness keeps us relaxed and joyous. Happiness is being contented and relaxed which would reward us with real affluence and serenity. Finding happiness in the happiness of others opens a floodgate of happiness at no cost.

2

<u>Friendship is the greatest treasure.</u>

Friends are like the Rock of Gibraltar.

- Murli Chari

Friendship is the best relationship in the whole world. They are better than blood relationships who treat as their right to question and advice expecting something in return. True friends are at our beck and call 24/7. Relatives on the other hand do not listen. They are always on the admonition mode. It is very aptly said that if you have one true friend that is enough even if the whole world is against you. Friends are the best shoulder to cry when we are in difficulty. To be a friend we need to be friendly with ourselves. A person who keeps himself aloof from others is not a good human being. Being a friend warrants lot of sacrifices. Friends indulging in binge drinking and dining need not be great friends. Friendship has to be nurtured through care and commitment. In friendship there are no expectations. The fair name of friendship has been stained as some people treat friends as ATM to withdraw money. Such friendships are doomed for failure right from the beginning. Such friends are parasites and a blot on the fair name of friendship. When everyone leaves you in the lurch friends give a firm support. Friends accept us as we are. We need not put up a façade. Friends are jewels in the crown. We need to adore our friends. Friends are our true mirrors. We must accept their criticism when we go astray. A true friend will never flatter. That is beneficial in the long run. Friendship does not differentiate between rich and poor. Money will never come in between friendship. Having committed and true friends is the greatest treasure.

3

Be a citizen of the universe

We are the gift of Universe.

- Murli Chari

Supreme Joy

We all have been created by the universe. There is no need to feel that we belong to a particular race, nation, religion, gender et al. The very reason there are so many violent carnages resulting in the killings of millions when we are biased. All violence emanates from biases, greed and judgement. We are bestowed with a cornucopia of blessings but alas we are squandering the riches. It is our social construct that is creating belligerence and needless devastation. Its time we create a world with no national boundaries paving way for an egalitarian affluent human society. We need to go beyond and become a citizen of the universe. With the science and technology growing by leaps and bounds days are not far off when inter-planet travel becomes ubiquitous. We dismiss some of the fantasies in the scriptures as myths but it could have been a reality in the bygone era. We should not confine ourselves to our planet earth. Most of the human beings are stuck in the medieval mind-set. To become a citizen of the world requires us to get out of the quagmire of many biases. We are all so caught in the commercial world we fail to appreciate the beauty of the universe. How wonderful it would be to witness 145 moons of Saturn as at present we have a solitary moon. Also, it would be marvelous to watch 95 moons in the sky of Jupiter. The very thought is exciting. Now is the time to dismantle nations and explore the sprawling universe. We need to explore all the wonders of the universe. The reason of existence of the vast universe is to become as big as the universe.

4

Enjoy life without feeling guilty and getting attached.

Attachment creates misery.

- Murli Chari

We should enjoy life to the hilt. There is no need to feel guilty. The ascetics admonish people to avoid enjoyment. However, the caveat is to avoid getting attached to anything. When we possess things then the things possess us. Any loss or damage disturbs our peace of mind. If the universe wanted us to avoid enjoyment, then it would not have created so many myriad things abundantly. When we feel guilty while savoring something that creates stress and misery. Living life full of joy and enjoyment is the very purpose of life. Only thing to take care is to not commit to over-indulgence. Addiction is the anathema. Everything in moderation is what is required. While enjoying make sure you do not entertain any guilt feeling as that would create sinful feeling. Not enjoying life is going against the grain of nature itself.

5

<u>Life is the greatest teacher</u>

Life gives exams first and lessons after them.

Anonymous

What we learn in schools and colleges are pebbles compared to what life teaches. If we observe whatever is happening around us, we will become really erudite. We seldom forget what life teaches us. If we keep repeating the same mistakes we will not go ahead. The very purpose of life is to keep on learning even after we are through with formal education. The lessons we learn from life is very impactful. There are legions of great people who have no formal degrees but they learnt directly from life. All evolutions take place from the lessons life give us. There is an apt adage "Once bitten twice shy" which means we do not mostly commit the same mistakes. When the life gives us lessons it enhances our capacity to circumvent our problems. While we learn from formal education, we do so to clear the exams and getting good grades. On the other hand, whatever we learn from life the experience is firmly ensconced in our memories.

6

Relentlessly march ahead towards your destiny.

Awake arise and march on till you reach your goal. - Swami Vivekanand

Supreme Joy

First and foremost, thing is to have clarity about our purpose. Once our purpose is clear we need to relentlessly march on towards our goal no matter what. There is no point in getting down in an intermittent station when our ultimate station we covet is very amazing. Leaving our most coveted dreams in the lurch is colossal waste of energy. We should not squander our most precious resources. We need to enjoy our pursuit and make it very enjoyable. When we enjoy what we are doing then we do not feel the stress. Most people are miserable because they are in the wrong place for eking out a living. Our world would be a better place if each one of us did what they love doing. When we are doing what we love we are brimming with enthusiasm and ecstasy. We can do the impossible if we have unlimited enthusiasm for doing something. We are living in the best era of human existence and have ample of opportunities to do extraordinary things benefitting the large swathe of humanity. It's a once in a life time opportunity to live up to our potential. Each one of us has ample of talents which go untapped. We need to have immense self-belief. There are bound to be many hurdles enroute our destiny. Every time we fall, we need to get up and keep going. Our need to achieve our coveted dream we need to take all the pains along the way. We need to enjoy every moment along the way to destiny. When we are determined then the entire universe conspires to make our dreams come true as quoted in the legendary book Alchemist written by Paulo Coelho. While pursuing our goals we need to be oblivious to whatever is happening around us. Minor hiccups along the way should not bother us.

7

<u>The whole of universe is the common heritage of the entire humanity.</u>

Collectively everything belongs to all of us and individually to none. – Murli Chari

It's a travesty of justice that human beings have become braggadocios and hedonistics. Mahatma Gandhi aptly commented that "everyone's need can be met but no one's greed can be met". Even the filthy rich hanker after more and more thus putting stress on the planet. We have fragmented our universe due to national boundaries, different races, different religions, gender and other parochial boundaries. Once we coalesce all our energies, we can have the whole universe to ourselves. Our pygmy thoughts have thwarted from exploring the whole sprawling universe. We call ourselves advanced but so much is still available of the universe which can be added to our kitties. There is infinite supply of everything in the universe. It's time we form a world government having one religion to create a true paradise on planet earth.

8

<u>Treat failures as your bosom friend for great results.</u>

Failures are the intermittent stations enroute our destiny. – Murli Chari

Supreme Joy

Our path to success is paved with heartbreaking failures. They are the intermittent stations which have to be travelled. Like a train we do not get down on the intermittent station but travel to our destination. Failures are merely milestones which are part of growth. If we persist by getting up after we fall and start walking, we are certainly going to reach our destination. Failures must be accepted and new strategies have to be devised to change the path but keeping intact our destination. Most people give up when they fail rather than take a retreat and march on. As per the great statesman Winston Churchill "Success is nothing but marching from one failure to another failure with enthusiasm. Likewise, Thomas Edison invented electric bulb after failing ten thousand times. He famously said they were ten thousand steps and not failures. Successes make us haughty whereas failures make us humble and aids us in marching towards our coveted goal with vigor.

9

Break the fetters of all rules and superstitious beliefs

No laws are sacrosanct. – Murli Chari

To make phenomenal progress we need to break all the rules set by the society. We blindly belief in antiquated beliefs which sabotage our real goals and purpose. The burden of beliefs is so heavy that we are not able to fly in the skies. Our distorted belief system sets limitations to what we can achieve. It is like tying our body with iron ingots and enter the ocean. You are bound to drown due to this burden. As per Dr. George Bernard Shah the world progresses due to those mavericks who are unreasonable and do not get caught in the quagmire of social diktats as those who conform to societal rules remain mediocre. The constant bombardment of various media of negative news is besmirching our confidence as they indoctrinate false and obnoxious beliefs. We can make a fresh beginning for a wonderful life if we get rid of our false beliefs. Our beliefs are our blind spots choking our necks. Ominous beliefs about many things stymie us. We must slay the demons within us which emanate from our skewed beliefs. Most of the beliefs are tainted with superstition as many beliefs emanate from religions. Despite many beliefs being ominous we still persist with them. Beliefs are very insidious as they are irrational. We must question each and every belief before we embrace them.

10

<u>Spread joy and happiness</u>

Joy and happiness are the elixirs for brilliant life. – Murli Chari

We need to be the harbinger of joy and happiness. The very purpose of life is joy and happiness. When we spread joy and happiness in the world then our own joy and happiness become an avalanche of bliss. Joy and happiness do not require a dime. They create camaraderie and humanity. Joy and happiness create dopamine in the brain. Joy and happiness make our life purposeful and we become healthier. When every one of us embraces this policy, our world would become a great place to live. Those following this principle treat even a rank stranger as their buddies. Spreading joy and happiness leads to burgeoning happiness and joy within.

11

The whole world is ours as well as happiness.

Happiness is free and so also is the universe. – Murli Chari

At any given point of moment, we can have all the happiness to our heart's content. The whole world is ours if we treat every human being as our own selves. Just imagine the freedom we enjoy at any given point of time. The sprawling universe with all the marvelous celestial beings belongs individually and collectively to each one of us. The sun the moon the stars and the infinite universe is ours. It does not cost us a dime. Our own being is a magical and wondrous thing. Our body is a miraculous thing with trillions of cells keeping us healthy and happy. Our brain is much superior than the best of computers. If we are grateful to the generous universe then we can have anything we covet. We have access to everything but are thwarted by the commerce which demands a price from us. We hold on to our possessions at the cost of owning the whole universe. The whole existence is so beautiful and mirabilia that we are left with awe-inspiring feeling. If we besmirch the money-oriented system each one of us will be a billionaire. We need to switch to value-oriented paradigm which is based solidly on humanitarian value.

12

We all are miniature divinity.

The spark of divinity is hidden in our hearts. – Murli Chari

Supreme Joy

If we consciously think we would realize that we are miniature gods. We have immense potential to reach the apogee of grandeur. We need to do away with our worries, doubts, insecurities and fear to realize godhood. Millions upon millions are living like zombies and will go to their graveyards without realizing their full potential. We need to harness all our latent talents to become miniature cosmos. Just imagine the greatest miracle of our mind, body and spirit making us awe-inspired. Every organ is a great wonder. Many of us do not realize what mirabilia we are. Millions take birth and die with lot of song left in them. We need to nourish the divine within us. Trillions and trillions of cells are there in our system. Divinity consciousness is present in each one of us. Crass commercialization has rendered us as mere commodities. Each one of us is worth trillions and trillions of dollars' worth. Most of the violence is unwarranted. If we live in harmony and peace, we can create paradise on earth.

13

<u>We need to choose better over bitter.</u>

We can either get better or bitter. Choice is entirely ours. – Burk Hedges

Every moment we have a choice to become better or bitter. It is all about our attitude. We need to stop complaining, condemning and criticizing. If we choose these negative attitudes, we become bitter. Better is always better and bitter is always bitter. If we focus on better, we will grow exponentially. If we prefer better then with each passing moment, we become great. Bitterness may emanate from envy, anger and frustration. On the other hand, better comes from celebrating others prosperity and successes. Prefer better to bitterness as that will burgeon affluence, happiness and peace. Bitterness exacerbates misery and better leads to bliss. It is a perennial process of getting better and better with each passing moment. Its only a matter of choice. Millions upon millions are preferring bitter over better and that is the reason there is sorrow in the world. It is rampant and ubiquitous. When each one of us chooses better than the world will become a better place. Bitter affects all the parties in a negative way and better also impacts all the parties in a positive way.

14

<u>Optimism is the key to success.</u>

An optimist sees opportunities in a problem and the pessimist sees problems in every opportunity. – Anonymous

For us to accomplish the impossible we need to be very optimistic. Optimism keeps our morale very high and keeps our spirits soaring. The moment we are optimistic we create a very salubrious and congenial atmosphere in our minds leading us to massive action on the ideas we contemplate. We develop a world class attitude which is very helpful in marching towards our coveted destiny. Thomas Edison, Jamshedji Tata, Newton, Benjamin Franklin, William Shakespeare, Dr. George Bernard Shah, Abraham Lincoln, Dhirubhai Ambani, Narayan Murthy, Kroc of McDonalds, Walt Disney, Bill

Gates, Elon Musk, Warren Buffet and legions of others saw opportunity where none saw. These people were the Avant Garde in the virgin fields. This one attribute will go a long way in helping us reach our dream goals. On the other hand, pessimism negates all the other good qualities. Millions of millions of people due to pessimism make their lives miserable and live an ordinary and mundane lives. Pessimism is like living in a claustrophobic dungeon cursing and blaming others and stars. This will leave us in the lurch and be a liability to ourselves and the world at large. It is just a matter of choice but it makes all the difference between success and failure.

15

Universe is divinity

Most of the ideas about divinity is gibberish. – Murli Chari

The whole of universe sprawling across infinity is divinity itself. All the other things are just symbols for our benefit. Most of the ideas of divinity are figment of imagination and hallucination. How can there be a plethora of gods of different religions? It's just absurd. Every religion claim that the universe was created by their gods. This notion leads to hatred and violence. Every religion is rigid and intolerant. The present chaos and carnage are due to the mushrooming of religions. If everyone accepts that the universe is the divinity then there would be no bone of contention. The violence perpetrated in the name of God and religion is ridiculous as whether they have the permission from the so-called god to commit carnage in his name. If he permits violence in his name then he ceases to be sacrosanct and not worthy of worship. If we foster humanity, then that would be the greatest tribute and service to the divinity. The universe comprising all the celestial bodies, our planet earth with its gorgeous cornucopia of beautiful things is just beyond our wildest dreams and imaginations. It's the evolution of universe that all life came into existence on our planet. The whole of universe is the heritage of all humanity. We are also part of divinity. We have to evolve to become as infinite as the universe itself. Not for nothing the universe is so mysterious, infinite and gorgeous. We have to rise above the mundane and the hedonistic materialism to become part of the universe. Too much of societal pressure is pushing everyone into the rat race. If we really want to become divinity, we have to free ourselves from ego, anger, hatred, lust, envy and greed. For humanity to burgeon we have to promote camaraderie. Just for few silver dollars we are losing the greatest treasure which is available in abundance for the whole of humanity.

16

Treat every living thing as well as non-living thing with the reverence due to divinity.

Honor life and celebrate. – Murli Chari

Every life form is the gift of universe as well as divinity. When we revere even a rock, we assure affluence for us. Even plants, trees, animals respond to love. The whole of existence is energy and connected with each other. We breath the same air and share all the existence with each other. When we treat everything with respect, we raise our level of consciousness. Treating every living and non-living thing with great reverence great feeling and love burgeon in our being helping us attract affluence. When we are full of love, happiness and compassion we live life of great bliss and peace. We can share only what we have. We can share love if we are filled with love. We cannot share love if we are filled with hatred. To truly evolve we need to revere each and everything in the environment. If we demean other living and non-living things we also are demeaned.

17

<u>Mind, body and spirit are indistinguishable.</u>

Everything in the world is energy at the atomic level. – Murli Chari

To our perception we feel as if mind, body and spirit are separate. However, on the energy and consciousness level they are integrated. Everything is energy at the atomic level. They look solid but they are bundles of energy. All the three elements together form our personality. Once we accept this fact then we can be the fountainheads of joy and happiness. All our body looks solid but once we keep on going deeper and deeper everything is energy. We are made of trillions and trillions of cells. They all coordinately work to keep our system working. Fear, worry and anxiety bring down our morale and we are not able to work at our peak tempo. On the other hand, if we are happy, we do wonders as all the systems work at their peak. We need to align our mind, body and spirit to do wonders. We are microcosm doing the same wonders as macro cosmos. Though the mind, body and soul look separate they are part of the same ecosystem. If we treat mind, body and spirit separate then we are the losers. On the other hand, if we treat them as one unique system then we will benefit abundantly. Great people like Abraham Lincoln, Mahatma Gandhi, Dr. Martin Luther King Jr., Dr. Nelson Mandela, Dalai Lama and the legions of others took advantage of this trinity. Its like a tripod which is supported by all the three legs. Even if one is defective the tripod will fall out of balance.

18

We need to keep on killing ourselves to grow

Kill the Buddha if you find him on the road. – Anonymous

Each moment is an opportunity to learn something new. For this to happen we have to break the concrete ensconced in our being. All the old beliefs avert us from becoming great. The very purpose of life is to keep on learning and unlearning. All the beliefs are to be besmirched as however good they maybe they have short shelf life. Most of the beliefs are borrowed and not proved with evidence. The antiquated and archaic belief systems are the cause for many avoidable troubles. The dichotomous beliefs lead to carnage and bloodshed. Change is necessary for evolution. Our universe is evolving every moment. Most of us are believing outdated beliefs leading to our abysmal nadir. As per great and intelligent philosopher J Krishnamurthy we have to die every moment to grow. All the great people in different domain keep learning and changing their belief system to keep pace with changes in the world. In these days of galloping science and technology most of the beliefs become stale in the next moment. Perennial learning will keep us lean and mean enabling us to strive in these days of fast pace. Beliefs make us rigid leading to destruction. The more flexible we are the more alive we are. When we entertain the same thoughts, we continue to live in the past with its obnoxious and ominous portents. We human beings have phenomenal power to live a brilliant life if we are cautious in embracing the right beliefs. Human brains have more synapses than all the stars and celestial bodies in the universe as per scientific research. This is really a great gift if we break the old and outdated belief systems and replace them with new beliefs. We need to be like nomads as far as our thoughts are concerned. We empty garbage bins everyday but do not throw away the filth accumulated in our system.

19

<u>Relax, everything is fine</u>

A relaxed mind conquers all. – Murli Chari

With constant flurry of thoughts playing havoc with our being it is difficult to focus on the most important task at hand. A relaxed mind creates magic. In the hustle bustle of daily life, we are unable to reach the apogee of glory. A relaxed mind enhances the capability and competence of our mind to work effectively. A muddled mind messes up everything, creates stress and chaos. Imagine a plethora of controls a pilot has to handle while flying a plane and his mind is not focused. He has to be very relaxed to handle complex procedures as the lives of hundreds is in his hands. If we are perturbed, stressed up and confused lacking clarity we are not in a relaxed mode which is the key to great and resounding success. A chaotic and stressed mind presses the panic buttons too soon resulting in disaster and ominous consequences. On the other hand, the adage "Relax, everything is fine" enhances our ability to do wonders. A cool calm and composed mind cures crisis. Many disasters can be averted if we remain relaxed as that makes us intrepid. When we are relaxed many of the problems can be solved. Ideas come gushing. A relaxed mind gets done humongous tasks quickly which a disturbed mind takes hours. Whenever we notice stress cropping up, we need to reassure ourselves by saying "Relax, everything is fine." It is ubiquitous to see many of the offices fitted with air conditioners as that keeps us relaxed when the situation frays our nerves making us frazzled for frivolous issues. Swami Sukhabodhananda wrote a legendary book "Mind, Relax". Reading that book would make you understand the supreme importance of remaining relaxed. Virtues of remaining relaxed is humongous. Remaining relaxed throughout the day is as good as meditation. It is beneficial for all. "Relax, everything is fine" is not a mere wishful thinking but a pragmatic wisdom. It helps in keeping under reins the adrenalin rush which makes us to fight or flight approach a zilch. Being relaxed keeps our expectations low as huge expectations lead to stress and frustration.

20

<u>Money is like a river</u>

Money needs to flow like a river and that is why it is called currency. – Murli Chari

When money flows it creates prosperity and happiness enroute. If it is hoarded it becomes stagnant and moribund. When money passes through many hands it creates goods, services and revenue to millions. Thousand rupees can create billions of rupees depending upon its velocity. A circulating system of money is good for the health of the economy and people. When money is hoarded it becomes vulnerable to theft and violence. On the other hand, spending money creates a salubrious and affluent society. It is a mistaken notion that when we spend money, we are squandering our wealth. On the contrary when we allow the money to flow, we create prosperity to many as well as ourselves. My friend, philosopher and guide Shubha Baldota has written a wonderful booklet "A thought for your penny" on the real significance of money and why it should keep flowing. We should bless the money when we spend or lend as that burgeons our wealth and that of others. If we keep the money in the locker, it would remain the same as far as its value is concerned and if it circulates it multiplies millions of times. There is a mistaken belief that money spent is money lost. Let the floodgates of money flow like a river then there would be immense benefits for all. All the crimes committed for earning will be put to an end. Money is neutral and it will take on the meaning given by us. The money going to charity will be greatly beneficial and going towards unethical things will vitiate the climate. We need to teach this philosophy in the schools, colleges and institution. Once this philosophy pervades in the world most of the intractable problems can be solved. Too much of importance to money needs to be reined in. It can do wonders as well as wreak havoc. Choice is entirely ours. Blind love for money is fraught with ominous portents. Money is the most potent weapon to create egalitarian affluence with peace and bliss. The currencies across the globe should contain the picture of divinity. That will dissuade people from abusing the money. There are many family disputes due to money as most of us fail to understand money correctly. Let us rejoice our lives by creating a paradise on earth.

21

<u>The virtues of discipline are overrated.</u>

Love is better than discipline. – Murli Chari

Rather than sticking thickly to discipline we need to love whatever we are doing. Discipline has a negative connotation. We feel as if we are put on treadmill. Most of us dread adhering to disciplines. As per Robin Sharma the legendary author discipline is tough love. If we have such an attitude then we will feel better. We need to resort to self-discipline rather than external discipline as we feel we are being incarcerated. When external discipline is imposed, we try to rebel against that. If we do everything lovingly there is no need for discipline. Discipline in the way we perceive is obnoxious and inimical. In most places where time discipline is there, there is lack of work discipline. When children are reared with love, discipline is not needed. Discipline is the most abhorred virtue. We reluctantly follow them. In such cases discipline is counterproductive. In nature everything evolves smoothly. The very word discipline smacks of terror. Rather than implementing discipline we need to persuade and inspire people to do their best in all endeavors. Discipline in military is understandable as they have to put up with arduous tasks while dealing with enemies. In other spheres cajoling is much better. As per Osho discipline comes from the root word disciple means who is on the learning mode.

22

<u>Quit doing what you dislike</u>

Love what you do and do what you love. – Anonymous

There is no point in doing what you dislike as that would create misery for you and others as well. Discipline creates stress and discomfort for us. Millions upon millions suffer due to imposed discipline. If we allow people to do what they love then there would be bliss and rewards around. When we do things grudgingly then we are causing misery to ourselves and others as well. A disgruntled employee will not do good service to customers who is the purpose of any business. Most of us grudgingly continue working in the cul-de-sac jobs just to eke out a living. It is better to quit dead-end jobs and do something

Supreme Joy

for which we have enough flair and panache. There is a plethora of examples where people have reached the apogee of glory. All those who have reached acme of fame, fortune and success do what they love. Not quitting from the job or vocation we abhor we are living in a veritable hell. It is a colossal waste of life if we continue with the jobs we hate so much. We are squandering the talents we have been bestowed by the universe. It is a humongous loss to the world when people are in the wrong place. In the initial stages it would be difficult to earn handsome money doing what we love but persistent effort would attract immense abundance and bliss. Its time we encouraged all the people to do what they like as that is the panacea for many ills afflicting the human society. There is risk involved in doing what we love but the rewards are way beyond our wildest imaginations. There are legions of glaring examples of those who wrote their names in the firmament like Bill Gates, Dhirubhai Ambani, Tatas, Elon Musk et al. There are legions of such greats who followed their bliss that it would need a voluminous book on that. When we do what we love then our levels of morale and enthusiasm are at the peak.

23

<u>Doing a job for making a living is a cardinal crime</u>

Working on a job will give you a living and working on oneself creates a fortune. – Jim Rohn

Doing a 9 to 5 job is squandering our precious resources. In a job we do not take full responsibility of our lives. We do only that much which would keep our jobs intact. In a job we do not harness our full potential which each one of us has in abundance. We tend to focus only on doing the job in a perfunctory manner. When we are on our own, we make best use of our latent talents. Job may give us security but we live a life of misery. Bill Quain in his incredible book Overcoming Time Poverty has quoted that we work for forty years and get 40%. Whereas if we take the risk and do what we love we can make a fortune in 4 years that too enjoying all the freedom of time and money. Time has come now that each one of us becomes an entrepreneur rather than an employee. This augurs well for the entire mankind. If we besmirch this employment method and replace it with entrepreneurship then everyone of us would be a billionaire. It has been observed that in jobs people watch clock and while away their time rather than adding value to customers employers and ourselves. Those who are in jobs are unable to fathom the depth of their personality. Each one of us immense talents which will take many lifetimes to harness. Most go through the motion living a mundane and regimented lives and go away with lot of song left in them. Or else we can have partnership models where people are paid for the results rather than time spent. Most of the employees do their work grudgingly rather than enjoy doing what they are doing. This job culture has left many people high and dry with no joy in their lives. To be on our own is the best option though there may be many struggles before we succeed. Human life has taken billions of years to evolve and we are squandering that in frivolous way. Most of us are living in a dungeon and claustrophobic eco-system but do not have the courage to come out of the quagmire. It is like a frog which is living in a lukewarm water and does not come out. Slowly the temperature increases and the frog dies. Same is the case with human beings as they are reluctant to come out of the comfort zone.

24

We are all immortals

We are all made up of energy and so we are eternal beings. – Murli Chari

Death is a misnomer. We are all immortal beings with infinite time to live and do things we are capable of doing. It is our ego that makes us scared of death which is a myth. Our human being is full of energy as at the atomic level we are nothing but energy. Scientists say "Energy can neither be created nor destroyed." Even our thoughts are mystical as we do not know its source. When we die where does all the energy go? It will go to the ether medium. It is still a mystery what happens after death of physical body. As thoughts are intangible, they may continue to live even after physical death. Human life is such a miraculous thing that science would invent something through which we will become immortal. Science and technology have so much potential that everything is possible. Nothing is impossible for the human ingenuity. We have been conditioned to think that we grow old and die. If we think that we are immortal then we will be immortal. At the atomic level we are all made up of energy. A quantum leap in this regard will turn everyone into an immortal being.

25

Charity brings affluence

Generosity is the key to abundance. - Murli Chari

Contrary to popular belief that when we spend money, we lose our wealth rather splurging money creates affluence for all. We need to do charity for the sake of our own bliss and overall egalitarian affluence. We will enjoy immense happiness when we prop up other people. Warren Buffet, Bill Gates, Tatas, Azim Premji and a legion of others have done lot of charity and still they have immense wealth. When we do charity, we create a magnet in our being to attract more wealth. The beneficiaries of our generosity bless us and that brings more affluence to us. Our wealth should be allowed to flow like a river as that would attract more wealth to us. When we hoard wealth there is a growing anxiety in us to safeguard it from the robbers. The more tight-fisted you become more the anxiety. When we splurge, we create affluence for thousands and to ourselves. USA is very prosperous because it is a spending economy which creates lot of opportunities for others to become wealthy.

26

Exams are scams as they hardly add value

Supreme Joy

Exams are the greatest obstacle on way to acquiring knowledge. – R.K. Narayan, legendary author of Guide, Malgudi Days and many more

When the objective is to clear the exams then students do rote learning and prepare at the last moment. On the other hand, acquisition of knowledge lays emphasis on slow learning with an intent to understand. Of late, many students acquire lot of degrees but they know very little. In the practical life, it is the knowledge that stands in good stead. Acquiring knowledge makes us a very matured personality. The purpose of human life is to acquire knowledge for knowledge's sake and not for eking out an existence. It is real joy to learn with understanding. We are happy to the brim when we know things thoroughly. Preparing for the exams creates stress whereas seeking knowledge is an enjoyable activity. Human societies should create an environ for gathering knowledge rather than procuring degrees by resorting to rote learning. When we resort to cramming and pass the exam, we cannot fly an aero plane. For flying we need immense knowledge and practice. All human endeavors require knowledge. Rote is of no use except for passing the examination. Such degrees are scrap and knowledge a precious diamond. This exam pattern compels certain students to cheat. On the other hand, there is no external authority to gauge our understanding. Knowledge enhances our confidence and maturity. Knowledge makes us a great citizen and is beneficial to us as well as others. To acquire knowledge outside the regimented curriculum of the formal education we have to read books which are not part of regular format. Mirza Ghalib, Sant Kabir, Shakespeare were very knowledgeable and are still relevant though they did not have lot of formal schooling. Same goes with Thomas Edison and Albert Einstein. They were branded as dumb-headed. Henry Ford the pioneer of cars was not having a degree to flaunt. If we lay more emphasis on acquiring knowledge rather than degrees the world would be a different place. Knowledge is the elixir of life. Knowledge makes us very discerning, gentlemen and gentlewomen.

27

Loafing around and pampering ourselves are good for us.

Self-love ensures love for others. - Murli Chari

Working hard for a living is bunkum and gibberish. Only those who are lazy invent energy-saving devices which greatly benefit millions. Microsoft office is such a great boon that they save lot of time, money and energy. In the excel lot of formulae makes calculations very easy. The founder Bill Gates was a college drop-out and so also was Steve Jobs the legendary and maverick entrepreneur. Loafing around makes us very relaxed and, in that state, we help our brains and minds to create and innovate may wonderful things. Pampering oneself makes our morale very high and we in turn add immense value to millions. The society drubs people who are laid-back and look for smart way to do things. Chester Carlson was a librarian who had to copy many texts for many people who needed important texts. In order to save time and effort he invented Xerox machine. That has proved to be a great boon. We need to encourage people to laze around and pamper themselves as something good will come out of that. Most of the inventions have been the result of lazing around. The whole evolution of mankind has been due to them inventing easier ways to do things. When we are lazing around and pamper ourselves our minds are very much relaxed which enables us to do phenomenal things. Its brain over brawn. Using our brains and minds are the laziest things ensuring great inventions and discoveries. Just slogging and working for 12 hours at a stretch does not amount to much. However, working for just a couple of hours in a relaxed manner produces miraculous and phenomenal things. Thomas Ferriss in his book Four Hour Week recommends working less and less and achieve more and more by resorting to short-cuts. With rapid progress in science and technology it is possible to work less and achieve more in a relaxed manner.

28

<u>Rules are for the dumb</u>

Gold makes the rules. – Murli Chari

Supreme Joy

Most of the rules prove to be obstacles in our growth. No doubt, certain rules are for the harmony of the society. We need to break the rules which are impediments. Dr. George Bernard Shah rightly said that only unreasonable human being can create value and those who conform to the societal diktats stagnate and do not add any value. Those who give excuses of rules are complacent and do not get out of the comfort zone. There is an adage "Gold makes the rule". The filthy rich get away with any flagrant flouting of the rules. It is only the not well- to- do get punished for their defiance of the rules. One more cliché is "No lock can hold against the power of Gold". The rich can use their clout to break the rules. Some are more equal before the law. Judicial system is bureaucratic rigmarole. The distorted and skewed judicial and police system are the reasons for much of injustice in the society. If each one of us behaves in a humanitarian way there would be peace and harmony in the world. Rules are truly good if justice system is impartial. More rules mean more corruption and abuse. Those who are in a position of power always try to exploit the hapless and underprivileged. Those who are endowed with power must act with understanding compassion and responsibility to implement the rules. It is a gauntlet to those in power must accept with nonchalance. All the rules are supposed to be exercised to keep the harmony and not to exploit the underprivileged. However, it has been found that power inebriates authorities and the result is obnoxious. Too many rules make people feel guilty and ominous. Many people pay two hoots to rules. Most people rebel against the rules which they find as an albatross. Voluntary compliance of rules burgeons humanity and the rules are complied with happily. Those who are powerful find it below their dignity to follow the rules. Legions of rules become ominous for the well-being of society. Rules are never followed in letter and spirit. Rules are only in the statute books. The very purpose of rules is not understood as people treat them as something not needed.

29

<u>We need to experiment with many things</u>

Supreme Joy

Variety is the spice of life- Anonymous

Living a stereotype life is both dull and drab. We must squeeze every ounce from life. For that we need to toy with many experiences. Experimenting with life brings the best out of us. We need to live a thousand lives in our lives. Living a secured mundane and regimented life is very boring and insipient. We must squeeze every ounce from our lives. Human life is so wonderful and immense that living the life the same way in and out of each day is a cardinal sin. The very purpose of human life is to experiment as Dr. Helen Keller advised that life needs to be lived like an adventure or nothing. The legendary author Timothy Ferris in his book "The four-hour work week" narrated his own life experiences of achieving multiple achievements by experimenting with his life. Jack of all trades and master of none is out of vogue. We can be masters in many domains. Jim Stoval who wrote The Ultimate gifts was an ace pilot, car -racer et al though he was blind. Many of us settle for a mediocre life though we have humongous talents. Late Shrikant Jichkar was a multi-talented personality. He was in the Guinness book of world records for procuring the greatest number of degrees. He was also a great expert of astrology and palmistry. AB de Villiers was a great international cricketer as well as international soccer player. There are legions of people who are good in dabbling with so many things with great elan and panache. Dr. Abdul Kalam toyed with many things with great success. We need to besmirch the belief that we can do few things with grand success. The amount of time we squander on worthless things like negative thinking, gossiping and condemning can be channelized to experiment with life and be opulently rewarded. Most of the people settle for mediocre jobs and thus miss the opportunity to grow by experimenting with many things. Every moment must be lived fully by sharpening our skills by experimenting with myriad things. Classic example of this is the legendary scientist, sculptor, artist Leonardo Da Vinci is very prominent. Live life as if there is no tomorrow. No human being can know when he is going to die. Even this moment could be your last. Most of us keep postponing our lives though the reality is always in the present. Making the most of each moment is really very rewarding.

30

Consistency is the virtue of an ass.

We need to keep changing our colors like a chameleon. -Murli Chari

If we are known to do the same thing day in and day out, we are caught in the rut. Most of us are consistent and so are predictable leading to stagnation. There is no point in being consistent as we hardly grow. To being consistent is choosing mediocrity. Unless we stretch our limits, we cannot grow. Growth is very vital. Without growth we are on the path to devolution. When we are consistent, we settle for mediocrity. On the other hand, a horse has multiple uses. It has speed, smartness and intelligence. Horses have been a great friend in wars and they are great race makers. An ass is useful only for carrying loads. It is the ally of washerman and does the same thing day in and day out. No disparaging the donkey which has evolved in a different way. Many of us do the same work consistently without any innovation and creativity. Following the same routine and regimen dulls and we are stagnant leading to moribund. We have to follow the kaizen to make incremental positive addition. We must break the daily routine and take a quantum leap creating wow experiences for all. Consistency may be a highly appreciated virtue as it becomes easier thing for the society but inimical for the individual. We need to be like a chameleon changing colors to camouflage to match the environment. Human beings are supposed to evolve with each passing moment or else they will become irrelevant. Consistency will inhibit us from doing great things. If we want to achieve phenomenal things then we have to forsake consistency. Consistency is like applying brakes when we are pressing the accelerator. That breaks the momentum and makes us frustrated. Consistency is akin to inertia and thwarts momentum leading to mediocre results. If we want to create a wonderful life then we have to swerve away from consistency. If we want to reach the apogee of glory, we have to besmirch consistency.

31

<u>Accept Challenges and risk failures</u>

Taking no risk is the riskiest thing. - Anonymous

We need to accept the gauntlet thrown by the existence as not doing that would stall our growth. Running away from challenges impairs our growth, confidence and chutzpah. By accepting challenges, we come out of our comfort zone. Without effort butterfly cannot come out of the chrysalis. Seeds need to break and die to become massive tree yielding flowers and fruits. The ultimate destiny of seeds, rivers and human beings is reaching the apogee of glory. Challenges bring out the best out of us. Challenges motivate the champions and breaks the diffident. Human beings would not have progressed so much without accepting challenges. Nature always keeps throwing

Supreme Joy

challenges towards every creature to enable them to evolve. Our recent life has been possible because geniuses accepted the gauntlet. Dr. Helen Keller though afflicted with so many handicaps lived an exceptionally great life ameliorating the lives of millions. Thomas Edison invented the electric bulb after failing hundreds of times. Where would have been we without this invention.? Wright brothers fought against many challenges to invent aero plane which has made travelling in the air so hassle free. We need to have temerity and indomitable courage to accept challenges. We cannot achieve much without accepting challenges. The Silk Yara tunnel rescue is one of the finest examples of how so many people put in efforts assiduously to save 41 workers who were trapped in the tunnel. It took 17 days to do the rescue act. In existence there are many challenges that come up to check for preparedness. So, we have to accept the gauntlet and come out from the quagmire. In life we have to take bold risks and fail. The more we fail the more we succeed. There is an adage "Bigger the failure bigger the reward." Our lives are like huge ships which is meant to weather the storm and conquer the sea and not to be safely anchored to the coast. Ships are not meant to be anchored to the shore but to venture into the high seas and vanquish the tempest. Our lives will be insipid dull and drab without challenges. Challenges bring out the best in us. We need to fully exploit our latent talent for our own benefits as well as for the entire humanity. Abraham Lincoln took up challenges with great temerity. He failed many times but never gave up.

32

<u>Rock the status quo.</u>

Kerry packer changed the cricket to a flamboyant style. – ICC

Kerry Packer broke the mold and changed the very format of cricket. He brought color dresses into the cricket game. Dr. Manmohan Singh as a finance minister brought in drastic changes and reformed the economy. The then P V Narasimha Rao gave free hand to Dr. Manmohan Singh. This rocked the status quo and lot of investments poured in. Status quo leads to stagnation and moribund. Once we take the initiative to roll on, we break the status quo and there is a cascading effect. All progress takes place by besmirching the status quo. We human beings have immense potential but we hardly harness our latent talents. We need great gumption and audacity to break free from status quo. All improvements and progress take place only on breaking away from status quo.

33

Be your own coach, mentor and trainer.

Being our own coach, mentor and trainer as we know ourselves thoroughly well. - Murli Chari

Having an external coach cost, us a fortune and still there is no guarantee that we would reach your coveted destiny. Furthermore, we are not sure we would be able to harness our full potential. Even the perceptions may differ and that would lay hurdles on the way. Being your own coach, mentor and trainer has many benefits as we are our own connoisseurs. We know ourselves thoroughly well. Our temperament, idiosyncrasy and attitude are different. We are the one who can perfectly judge our strengths and weaknesses. This saves lot of energy and time. In brief moment of time, we can mentor ourselves. Once we own up the responsibility we are on our way to the coveted destiny. We can rejoice, celebrate and enjoy every moment of coaching, mentoring and training. When we take our own responsibility then we cannot blame others.

34

<u>Laughter is the best medicine.</u>

Laughter is the rare virtue of human beings which can defuse many hostile situations. -Murli Chari

Laughter is one of the rarest features present in human beings. It cures many intractable illnesses. When we laugh, our whole being is transformed to divinity. When we laugh, we are transported to euphoria and exuberance. This is a rare and unique feature among human beings. When we frown many muscles are strained, whereas laughing involves very few muscles. Laughter is the greatest medicine which is free of charge. A person who can laugh at himself becomes the cynosure of all eyes. Laughing is contagious. It elevates our moods and leads to supreme bliss. Laughter builds friendship and bonding. The overall mood is euphoric. It removes bitterness and rancor.

35

Promote the interests of others

When we give others what they want then we will get what we want. – Murli Chari

When we are altruistic, abundance flows into us. When we are selfish and self-centered, we do not achieve what we are set out to do. When we go out and help others our own goals are easily achieved. When we help others, we are in a blissful state and anxious when we seek things for ourselves. If each one of us embraces this philosophy the world would be a paradise free from poverty, illiteracy and rancor. All violence and crimes are prevalent because we compete with others and scramble for things resorting to unethical and unscrupulous means. Most of the vexatious problems in the world are due to selfishness. Living and earning for a decent life without snatching things from others is fair. Best way to become very wealthy is to make others wealthy. It is basic human nature to being humane and help others generously. However, the popular belief is that in these dog eats dog days utter narcissism is the order of the day. Humanity is interwoven with each other. Together we can flourish and divided we perish. All the stress, strain, anxiety and tension are due to selfishness. When we pursue selfish pursuits, we are stressed up. On the other hand, when we are involved in helping others, we enjoy bliss. Also, it burgeons great human bonding.

36

Do not even trust yourself

Our trust in ourselves is due to our beliefs which may be skewed due to external influences. – Murli Chari

If we want to exponentially grow, we need to start not trusting ourselves as there may be many distortions in our belief systems. Most of our beliefs are indoctrinated by our well-meaning parents, loved ones, teachers and social leaders. In the formative years we are vulnerable to being easily impressed. We do not have the understanding to discern what is correct and what is not. Most of us live on borrowed wisdom which may be true or not. It takes lot of introspection and deep analysis to get to the bottom of the truth. We need to be ruthless in accepting the beliefs which have to be tested in the cauldron of reality. We have phenomenal potential which immensely rely on our correct conceptualization. We need to probe into everything before accepting the beliefs. Our destinies are shaped by our thoughts. That is the reason we should not blindly trust ourselves. If we profoundly research every belief, we entertain we will be able to trust ourselves and we would be highly rewarded. There are many blind spots in our brains and perceptions. We must take professional advice to resolve this issue. The more we question our own beliefs the more we will benefit. We are reluctant to get out of our comfort zone and that proves to be pernicious. The more you challenge your beliefs better it is for your growth. Be very ruthless with yourself as if you are slaying the demons within you. Most of the times we are our own enemies without realizing. 99% of the times we are wrong as we have to tolerate many things about others and accept things as they are. This is a strategy to accommodate others who are having negative traits. However, for our own benefit we have to ignore their flaws. We have to besmirch everything into smithereens as far as our distorted beliefs are concerned. That would be the greatest favor we would be doing to ourselves. Millions upon millions do not accept the gauntlet thrown by our blind spots. To challenge our own beliefs is very daunting but it's worth the effort to closely scrutinize our beliefs so that we have right kind of beliefs.

37

<u>Blend Materialism with spiritualism.</u>

Too much of materialism would lead to ennui and narcissism and too much spiritualism would make you anti-life. – Murli Chari

Supreme Joy

Too much of materialism is Narcissism and hedonism leading to ennui. Attachment to materialism would make us resort to unethical and unscrupulous means and there is no end to avarice. Millions of misguided people who perceive that materialism is all resort to devious means and crime to amass wealth. The scramble for material wealth has caused turmoil, carnage and devastation in the world. As per one report 70% of the court cases in India are due to property disputes within the family. Once materialism becomes an obsession, we are on the primrose way. Political corruption is due to the culture of the vultures. The rat race triggered by crass materialism has disturbed the harmony in the society. As per Brad of Avon the legendary William Shakespeare too much of anything is bad. On the other hand, spiritualism is diametrically opposite to materialism. Spiritualism burgeons humanity and camaraderie. One is very composed, compassionate and contented. The happiness emanating from materialism is ephemeral and limited in scope. On the other hand, spiritualism to my mind is to be considerate to other human beings as well as all the sentient beings, flora and fauna. It is eternal and infinite in scope. Materialism promotes self-centeredness whereas spiritualism promotes compassion, love and peace. Spiritual people are more altruistic and generous. All said we need to balance between materialism and spiritualism for supreme bliss. This is holistic approach. As Gautam Buddha rightly said that we need to follow the middle path. Too much of materialism may lead to plundering of the planet and disturbing the ecological balance. Spiritualism should not be stretched beyond reasonable limits to remain aloof and neglect our social obligations. Spiritualism to my mind is not the one usually thinks of as something to do with religion.

38

<u>Virtue is its own reward</u>

To expect something in return for exercising virtues is skewed

. – Murli Chari

Supreme Joy

The basic purpose of human life is to develop virtues. Developing virtues keeps us safe and away from committing sinister things. Having good virtues keeps us free from problems as most of the problems arise due to absence of virtues. Not having great virtues lure us into evil things without our knowledge. Virtues like honesty, punctuality, integrity, compassion, love, commitment and humanity are the real gems adorning our personality. When everyone commits to great virtues then we would have a paradise on earth and the criminal activities would not thrive. To have a salubrious world society each one of us has to have a treasure of virtues. Virtues are the real wealth rather than hordes of money, gems, glitzy gizmos et al. Pseudo wealth is no guarantee for a great life. A poor man full of virtues is far more valuable than a rich man full of evil habits. Having virtues may not guarantee great life but one is at peace since virtue is its own reward. As charity begins at home virtues have to be imbibed from the tender age. It is very difficult to harness great virtues at the stage of adulthood. Having great knowledge, wealth, and health may be of very little consequence if one lacks virtues. Lack of virtues is abominable as the innocent are always worried and fearful of the lurking danger. No human being is complete without virtues. Blatant neglect of virtues has made the world a veritable hell. To create paradise, we need to ensure that each one of us develops virtues and acts accordingly. Our children learn from how we act rather than from sermons as they are empty without action. The very essence of human life is a life lived on the basis of virtues. To salvage humanity from the morass we need to make sure everyone of us takes to virtue the sole savior of humanity and tribute to divinity. All the apostles of peace, progress, and prosperity were a paragon of virtues. Supreme joy that we are seeking emanates from practice of virtues.

39

<u>Balance your emotions.</u>

Emotions lead to commotion as they have no notion. – Murli Chari

A balance of emotions ensures bliss and harmony. Any disturbance in balance leads to

Supreme Joy

agony. Balancing emotions creates harmony. Emotion of love has to be nourished as it creates bliss, promotes healthy relationship peace and overall well-being. Emotion of empathy creates salubrious society. Empathy promotes humanity as we feel the pain of others including animals and plant. Emotions of hatred, fear, ego, anger, worry and envy are pernicious. These emotions sap our energy and pits us against others leading to squandering of precious resources. Aforesaid negative emotions are bound to be there in our being but they should be there in traces as predominance of these emotions can mar our lives. Most of the negative emotions suck our energies like a vampire. We need to keep our emotions on leash as untrammeled emotions can run amok and go berserk. Negative emotions have deleterious effect on our mental, physical, spiritual and humanitarian health. Positive emotions have a salutary effect on our health. The emotion of anger can make us behave like a beast. Most of the wars, crimes, violence and bestiality occur due to bad emotions. Positive emotions release good hormones like serotonin and dopamine and cortisol from negative emotions.   Negative emotions release the enzyme cortisol adversely affecting our health. Fear is one of the most dangerous emotions that paralyses our rational thinking. Our ancestors living in the dangerous jungles had the need for fear to protect themselves against furious and ferocious predators ready to ambush. Fear is a natural instinct necessary for survival. However, these days there are other reasons for fear which are not life-threatening but put us out of gear. Worry also is a negative emotion playing havoc without morale creating needless stress. For exuberance and supreme joy, we need to remain in a composed state of mind free from negative emotions and full of positive emotions.

40

Quit doing what you dislike

If we continue doing what we dislike we will get caught in the quagmire and never achieve what we dream. – Murli Chari

Supreme Joy

Most of the human beings are engaged in jobs which they hate. They remain in the jobs they hate as they have no other means to pay the bills. Each day they reluctantly go to their jobs they hate and remain in the prison of their own making. Millions upon millions are in a miserable state incarcerated in the prison of their own making. As most of us are caught in the prosaic and miserable jobs we hate there is misery prevailing everywhere. This is a loss to all the stakeholders as these people do not do their best. They do not follow their bliss. Following the bliss does not pay in the short run but in the long run it is very rewarding. One must follow one's bliss as that would create a tapestry of magic. People continue with their dead-end jobs as they have resigned to their fates believing that they do not have any choice. Unless you quit what you do not like you cannot fully realize your potential. Only under challenging and compelling situations we bring out the best in us. Otherwise, we do things mechanically and suffer needlessly. Once we are on our own, we can marshal all our latent talents for our own cherished goals. In a job most of the work is mundane, routine and boring as the work lacks creativity and imagination. There are very few who are in a job which is to their liking. Following the bliss may be less paying in the beginning but the gamble pays off. As per Bill Quain in his legendary book "Overcoming Poverty of Time" has explained the advantages of entrepreneurship visa-viz job. In a job it takes roughly around 40 donkey years to have our dream house, car etc. as compared to a roaring business in 4 years. Only those who dare can succeed. There is no point in slogging in a dead-end job to build the castles of others. We could as well work for our own little house where we are the emperors. In an entrepreneurial foray we have control over all the vital resources like money and time. We are all born emperors. So, there is no point in becoming bonded labors. Stay, you lose and quit you gain as far as dead jobs are concerned. In job our temperament is to pass time and do only that much where jobs are secure. In these dynamics all the stakeholders are losers. On the other hand, if everyone is an entrepreneur there would be phenomenal abundance in the world as everyone would fully harness his potential and would put heart and soul into what he is doing. If we get stuck in dead-end jobs, we continue to live in misery cursing everyone and eking out an existence. We are all ordained to become emperors and not slaves as doing what we abhor we are inviting life-long suffering.

41

<u>Doing a job is slavery and a crime.</u>

We are free birds and are not cut out for boring and mundane jobs. -Murli Chari

Only very few people fully realize their potential in a job. Millions grudgingly and reluctantly do their jobs creating misery for themselves and other stakeholders as well. Most of us do not put our hearts and souls into the work at hand. In freelancing we have control over all the vital resources like time and money as well as the freedom to put all our ideas to work. In a job one reluctantly gets up in the morning to go to the job. The ikigai or purpose is conspicuously missing. The spark is missing. Most of the heart attacks occur around 9 AM in the morning on any

Supreme Joy

Monday after a break in the routine. This is true as it is research finding. Magic happens when there is an alignment in mind, body and spirit focused on the job at hand. In a typical job employees are just whiling away their time and do very little which can keep their job. Jobs are being looked as a source of income to pay the bills. The commitment needed is missing. In the initial stages a job gives an assurance as the pay cheque arrives providing security. However, we are not able to fulfil our cherished dreams. That flow is missing which brings the best out of ourselves. When we are in an entrepreneurial enterprise, we provide jobs to many as well as there is no load on the job market. When we start a business initially there are many hiccups but we are able to not only provide jobs to others but we leave a legacy for the posterity. In a typical job we watch the clock to when it is time over for the day. We do not put our best. The whole society at large is at a loss. We human beings are born free and not designed to be a slave in a dead-end job. Only way to create a salubrious and affluent society is for each human being to be on his own. Very few people take ownership of the organization where they are

Supreme Joy

working. In a job we have very little freedom to put our ideas into practice as most of them are quashed by our bosses in the beginning throwing wet blanket on our aspirations. The nature wants us to shine with all the liberties like birds which soar into the skies. We human beings are not cut out for jobs. To have great affluence, freedom and peace is to start our own enterprise. Whatever may be our monthly salary we feel miserable as going through the routine is very treacherous. In a job there is a conflict of interest as employees want to work less and get paid more and the employers want the employees to get less and work more. This dichotomy is gravely affecting the productivity and quality. There is a war of conflict affecting human relationships. Doing the same thing day in and day out is very boring and mundane. It is the golden rule that we have to flourish or perish. Flourish we can in a business and sure way to perish is to carry on with a job. Now with tremendous scientific and technological matter gathering momentum there is humongous potential for everyone to start an entrepreneurial venture to fully explore the true potential of every human being. We must not fall into the quagmire of trouble due to the dragons

Supreme Joy

of money and time. In a job we are building the magnificent palaces and fulfilling the dreams of others who are very intelligent to use other people time and other people money. In an entrepreneurial venture we have the freedom to fan into different domains rather than sticking to the same boring and mundane domains. In freelancing we are able to explore and live thousand lives. We can take a break whenever we feel like and not like jobs where the employer decides when you can take leave. In a job all our creativities and imagination are nipped at the bud. We are like caged bird which gets lot of good things but have no freedom to fly. In a job we become bonsai trees which though look strong and sturdy but all its wings are clipped. No doubt, there are lot of risks and responsibilities in an enterprise but that brings the best out of us. The legendary author of Rich Dad Poor Dad famously quoted that we work and businessmen network. He also rightly pointed out that our worth is known by our network. More people we have in our close circle the better. Most of the problems and stress is because people are in a job they dislike but have to do to pay their bills. On the contrary, a businessmen have a swell of time enjoying every moment. The more he excels the more he flourishes. When we are on our own, we can grow exponentially helping others also excel and flourish provided he employs people as partners having a share in the profits and not as employees who are always miserable. If most of us are on our own the world would be a wonderful place where everyone is living up to his full potential. However, it would be better to create resources which can sustain us for two years else it would be hara-kiri. Everybody can be free without being great but no one can be great without being free as per legendary saint philosopher Khalil Gibran. Following one's bliss leads to immense freedom. Getting stuck in dead-end jobs is needless and self-defeating. No doubt, business entails many risks, uncertainties and inconsistent incomes. We are not sure how much and when we will get money to run our lives. Jobs are meant for the mediocre and passionless people. A business enterprise though very risky is much better than a boring job which sucks and no stakeholder is happy.

42

<u>Ways to become immortal.</u>

Death is a myth floated by society. We are all immortal beings capable of living without death lurking around the corner. – Murli Chari

At the outset ego invites mortality. Our egos are vaster than the universe itself though there are evidences that we are not even a grain of sand compared to the sprawling universe. Ego is just like a hard shell of a seed. A tree can germinate only if the seed breaks and becomes one with the whole. Ego is the worst enemy of perennial bliss and intense relationships. Ego developed as an instinct in medieval times as a defense mechanism. We were surrounded by wild animals read to prey on us. It was justified in those times. Ego makes us selfish. We can become great human beings if we shelve our egos. Ego, in fact, is high opinion of oneself and is very much concerned to protect us. It makes us think that we are something special. Ego blocks

Supreme Joy

the flow of knowledge, wisdom, peace, happiness, love and affluence. Ego can make us condescending. When the ego goes berserk it marauds everything on its way. Ego is like an untrammeled frenzied horse which runs amok. Ego treats everyone including our near and dear ones as enemies. When the ego reaches the zenith death is lurking around the corner. Ego makes us rigid which is death as per the maverick Osho. Once we break our egos, we become flexible and supple making us lively and friendly. Once we decimate our egos, we are open to everything and do not want to be superior to others. Once ego is taken out of the equation, we become immortal. Ego besmirches our energy and affects negatively our physiology consuming humongous energy; the vital force within us. It is egoless state that integrates us with the entire universe and divinity. Once we remove ego, we experience immense bliss and affluence. Our egos are the locks when opened triggers immense affluence, bliss and peace. When we get rid of our egos, we are able to harness our other faculties like awareness, consciousness, creativity, imagination, intuition and natural instinct. Life is reality and death an illusion and

Supreme Joy

hallucination. We are all the victims of victims comprising of our parents, siblings, teachers, friends, saints, governments, and ideologies of religion, economy and philosophy. When we commit ourselves to promote humanity, love and compassion we enter the realms of immortality. Purpose of life is a life of purpose sans ego. Ego acts like a break crushing our enthusiasm. Ego creates fear, insecurity, superiority complex, misery, stress, frustration, critical mindset and hosts of other negative things. Ego makes us an island amid the burgeoning societal avenues. The braggadocio treats everyone with disdain. Many of us have a conceited belief in their superiority which emanates from ego. Ego can be due to one's wealth, knowledge, religion, caste, race, gender and nationality. The indoctrination of thousands of years has made us believe in distorted and skewed doctrines which are at best superstitious beliefs. When we move beyond ourselves, we become the cynosure of the whole world thus become immortal. Ego promotes Narcissism and hedonism ultimately to ennui. Ego believes in more the better. It feels paranoid. It always looks at others as their bete noir. Ego squanders all the treasure trove of all resources on confining itself to self-aggrandizement. Name, fame, and fortune are all ephemeral and are ego-based. Ego is a self-imposed prison and the demon within which strangulates us. Oneness with all life ensures immortality. We can live forever by leaving a legacy of wisdom, culture and goodwill. There are legions of people who still live in the hearts of millions. When we besmirch ego and its allied allies, we besmirch death. Sooner or later mankind would discover the code to immortality. Certainly, ego if crushed and humility nurtured would go a long way to ensure immortality for human beings. Much of our energies are squandered in keeping alive our egos. When we integrate with the whole of universe, we are catapulted into divinity which is immortal. For the very purpose of human life is to reach the pinnacle of existence which is divine in nature. Ego is a thorn which needs to be removed to ensure happiness, peace and bliss. The flawed societal paradigm that we are bound to die is the cause of fatality. This can be reversed if we move beyond mind's machinations. Ego thinks that it alone can save us from enemies which are external. Selfishness which many consider normal creates immense stress, fear, anxiety and frustration moving us towards annihilation. A positive mental attitude, purpose, compassion, love, peace, generosity and selflessness lead to immortality. Selfishness makes us a paranoid as our goals require us to maraud others to enhance one's chances of success leading to immense wealth. This creates animosity with others including our near and dear ones. When we are selfless and generous we create wealth with peace assuring affluence for others as well and we pave the way for immortality.

43

<u>Charity brings affluence</u>

Charity is something magical as it creates affluence for those practicing it. – Murli Chari

Charity is the acorn engendering the massive oak tree of immense affluence. This is not something that needs to be resorted after taking care of all your needs. Even if we are left with meager resources, we need to practice it. Charity needs to be practiced without expectations of name, fame and good karma. Charity is one of the noblest of gestures. Charity done with good intentions and empathy is really commendable even if the amount is meagre. Charity needs to be given to the right person, for right reason and of the right kind. Charity is multi-dimension and can be powerful advice. Each one of us irrespective of our financial stature may deploy some part of our income towards charity as that would be a valuable contribution to the welfare of humanity. Foraying into charity without expectations keeps us exuberant and blissful. We need to make sure that we do not advertise our charitable activities as that would vitiate the essence of charity. Remaining anonymous would add grace to the act of charity. Charity is very much sacred and attracts immense happiness and phenomenal affluence as well. Charity is not an option but vital for maintaining the healthy balance in the society. Charity is much beyond parting with money and other things but involves many other things like sharing of our time, wisdom and knowledge. Being charitable in all spheres makes a colossus of a personality.

Charity done with a pure heart creates camaraderie with others. The famous adage "Charity begins at home" has profound meaning as we need to practice before we preach. Charity is the expression of gratitude to the benevolent Universe for making us rich enough to indulge in charity.

44

<u>We would immensely benefit from imbibing the qualities of dogs.</u>

Dog is an epitome of divinity. – Murli Chari

Dogs have many attributes worthy of emulation by us humans. One thing that dog has is its very faithful to its masters, warding off the suspicious people. Its faithfulness is unwavering indubitable and inimitable. Most of us desert the very people who pulled us out of the quagmire. Dogs are very enthusiastic and full of verve jumping when their masters come. Dogs are very friendly as well. They will never retaliate even if their masters ill-treat them. Their love is unconditional unlike human beings who always set preconditions for showing love. Dogs are very playful and shower unlimited love on their masters. We, human beings can abundantly learn from their canine friends. Human beings are lost in the quagmire of Narcissism and hedonism little realizing that supreme joy is free and at the disposal of all human beings who are wholly money-oriented. All the nature is free from the vampires of time and money which are proving to be the nemesis of humanity. Dogs rather the whole of nature is grounded in the now except human beings who are always worrying about the past or anxious about the future. Dogs do not get caught in the hallucinations as they do not have hubris.

45

Exams are a big scam ruining innocent human beings.

Acquire knowledge without bothering about exams. – Murli Chari

The purpose of exams when it was devised may have been genuine and adorable. However, over a period of time got degenerated and have become useless ritual as students cram to get through the exams without acquiring knowledge which is the true pursuit. There is a famous saying that teachers memorized the syllabus and downloaded it to the students who in turn vomited on to the answer -sheet without acquiring any sliver of knowledge. Most of us have been programmed to prepare for the exams and get good marks rather than focusing on acquiring knowledge which prepares us to do our best in the world to create wow experiences for many. Knowledge helps us in understanding the dynamics of how the world works. Exams create stress and anxiety without adding anything much towards knowledge. It has been observed that many gold medalists were found to be worthless in the real life. Now students are chasing degrees as they are more important in the market fetching them fabulous salaries. That is the reason students either mug up or try methods to get good marks including copying. Some students even go to the extent of tracing the examiners to manipulate through bribing to get good marks. Exams are a bundle of contradictions. The legendary author Late R K Narayan said "exams are the greatest obstacle on road to acquiring knowledge." Even the evaluation is arbitrary as valuers have different methods to give marks. If the same answer sheet is given to different evaluators different marks will be given. Exams must be given immediately after the lessons are given else it turns out to be rote learning. We need to encourage students by sowing the seeds of curiosity as that enables self-learning. The very purpose of education is to help students learn, know and think. Many great geniuses like Thomas Alva Edison, Albert Einstein and legions of others were declared dull students. Careers of many students have been besmirched due to faulty education system. It has been found that many distinguished scholars failed miserably as they did not have practical knowledge. True knowledge liberates a person and makes him more tolerant of many differences in many strata of world society. The purpose of education is to create great human beings who can shape the world. We should not confine acquisition of knowledge to making a living. Many people less endowed with degrees have risen to the pinnacle of glory. Its time we revamped the education system which helps human beings to live a worthwhile life adding immense value to millions as well as impact positively the world. Learning without the botheration and anxiety of exams would be a lot more fun. Learning with joy enhances the knowledge assimilation.

46

Loafing around is fun

Being serious all the time makes our lives miserable. – Murli Chari

Wandering aimlessly to enjoy the scenery is really very enjoyable pursuit. The cohorts of martinets eulogize the importance of slogging with their own axes to grind. Those who deploy capital expect their employees to slog and make money for them. Not everyone who loafs around is a responsibility shirker. Those who loaf around come up with brilliant ideas as they believe in smart work. Loafing around does away with stress and also rejuvenates us. However, full time loafing is inimical. Loafing around with friends does not only enhances knowledge but makes one affable to all. It also provides immense pragmatic knowledge. All work and no play makes Jack a dull boy is a very famous adage with immense wisdom. To know things first-hand loafing around is a boon. Loafing around does not mean indulging in binge eating and binge drinking. Loafing around should be with a purpose. It brings a load of cheerfulness and playfulness in life. In the absence of this life becomes insipid, boring, mundane and lackadaisical. Three cheers to loafing!!!

47

<u>Rules are for the morons</u>

Most of the rules are framed by the oligarchs. - Murli Chari

Supreme Joy

Rules are framed by the autocrats and plutocrats to rule the masses. More often than not, venal and criminals frame the rules which are flagrantly flouted by the set of rogues. Rich people indulge in wanton breaking of rules and get away. Only the masses are punished for the misdemeanor. In the absence of expeditious justice deliverance system , crimes flourish in the society making a mockery of rules. Rules which are just must be followed. Minor peccadillos can be condoned. Hardly few follow the rules in letter and spirit. Many rules framed in the bygone era needs to be modified to make them in sync with the current trend. Legions of rules have become archaic. Human relationships are more important than rules. Most rules are broken with gay abandon as they are very difficult to follow. There is a plethora of rules of which people are ignorant. It is humanly impossible to know all the rules which are there in the society. Any punishment proves to be counterproductive as they make the offenders more hardened criminals. It is human tendency to follow the path of least resistance. For example, it is ubiquitous to find the violation of dowry act which prohibits demanding dowry which is a scourge in Indian society. Even the most educated class transgress the rules. Use of obscene and abusive language is prohibited in India but citizens profusely use abusive words in public. A conscientious citizen does not need any rules as he is very humane to the core. Most of us find it cumbersome to follow the rules. Rules become irrelevant in the absence of a fast and just judiciary. Rules are for the morons emanate from the fact that the victims rarely get justice in the current times. That is the reason goons go on merrily flouting the rules. There is an adage that "Gold makes the rules" Most of the rules are written in cryptic manner to enable the rulers to snub their opponents and keep the rulers safe. Rules smack of authoritarianism. Rules have spawned many crimes. Those at the helm of the affairs use the ruse of rules to keep the opponents and masses under their thumbs. The rich and mighty have the upper hand as far as the rules are concerned. Politicians enjoy impunity as far as the adherence of rules go. Rules which are ambiguous and full of riddles are exploited to further the cause of political corruption. More the rules more the corruption. Rules need to be written in layman's language lest they are used to extract a pound of flesh. Lawyers thrive as the rules are written in a complicated manner. Compassion and wisdom of the yore better serve the purpose of promoting harmony in the society. Rules create bureaucratic rigmarole to promote corruption and inefficiency. We must understand that rules need to be simple, flexible and humane as they need to help human beings. Let us promote humanitarian values, wisdom, empathy and camaraderie.

48

<u>We need to experiment with many things.</u>

We need to break the belief that jack of all trades and master of none to blossom in life. – Murli Chari

Human life is really miraculous and endowed with a treasure trove of talents. We need to live a thousand lives in our lifetimes. For that to happen we need to foray into many arenas. There is a plethora of live examples of multi-faceted personalities like Leonardo Da Vinci who excelled in many fields as also Benjamin Franklin and our own Dr. Abdul Kalam. There are many other distinguished personalities who excelled in everything they took on. This distorted and skewed thinking is ubiquitous and we have been brain-washed to believe that we can be good in only one thing. Universe is a sprawling thing that inspires us to become a colossus. The secret to be masters in various domains is to focus on what we are doing at the moment. With the advent of internet, super-speed computers and artificial intelligence now it is possible to excel in many disciplines. We give undue importance to specialization. We need to pulverize into smithereens the skewed philosophy one cannot be good at many things. We have been programmed to think that to become experts in a myriad domains is foolhardy and impossible. Once we believe and accept that we can be experts in many fields we create many dimensions and the universe marshals all the resources to make it a reality. All the limiting beliefs firmly ensconced in our psyche are inherited from the indoctrination of well-meaning parents, friends, teachers, governments, idols, media, scriptures and religious heads. We need to know our blind spots and do whatever needs to be done to accept that we can do many things. Human brain, mind, awareness and consciousness have phenomenal capacity to learn and store humongous information, knowledge and wisdom. Scientists as well the legendary Acharya Rajneesh aka Osho say that there are more synapses in our brains than the celestial bodies. One human brain can contain all the libraries in the world as per Osho. It is our negative emotions of fear, doubts, superstitions, illogical concepts and ego that block all the knowledge and abundance. We need to keep on raising our bars to perennially excel and keep the momentum gathering pace at very moment. A laser-like focus and mindfulness work like magic. Social conditioning has clipped our wings and rendered us as bonsai tree of the oak kind. We need to expand our horizons and take a leap of faith to be experts in many fields. We need to do it for ourselves rather than to flaunt it to the society. We need to be impervious to the negative emotions, ridicule, and criticism. When the purpose is clear things will fall in place. Everything starts from our self-belief. In the modern era with lot of technology and knowledge being an expert in many fields is a child's play. Our commitment, focus, determination flexibility, knowledge, wisdom patience and perseverance make all the difference to attain proficiency in an array of domains. Let us throw lock, stock and barrel the distorted notion that we cannot excel in more than one field. As per the legendary author Napolean Hill "Whatever we conceive and believe we can achieve". Even if we fail, we would have walked thousands of miles. Every human being is like an onion in a sense that if we keep on peeling new layers appear. This is the recipe for supreme joy. We need not take anything very seriously. We can enjoy the journey without getting fixated over our goals.

49

<u>Consistency is the virtue of an ass</u>

Supreme Joy

To be consistent means we lose our charm. – Murli Chari

Many people keep doing the same things in the same way eventually getting bored with the routine and mundane. As per kaizen daily small improvements will make us formidable. We need to be creative and innovative to excel and enjoy. That way we are on the flow and are exuberant. We enjoy doing things and our lives become very euphoric. While we are consistent, we become predictable and get stuck at one place. It becomes very difficult to come out of the rut. Being stuck in the rut makes us mechanical and we become complacent. There is no progress when we become predictable. We go on the autopilot. It is very difficult to get rid of our mechanical and boring habits. Consistency kills all creativity, innovation and enthusiasm leading to stagnation. There is total lack of verve and enthusiasm leading to moribund. We become listless and lack vibrancy if we become consistent. Only dumb-witted become consistent. It is necessary for us to keep changing to be on the path to evolution. We human beings have become what we are today because of challenging the status quo. We need to keep challenging ourselves now and then to hone our skills. When we are inconsistent there is phenomenal potential for growth. We are programmed to evolve but consistency is the dampener and spoilsport. The great inspirational leader Jim Rohn famously quoted "If we work on the job, we make a living and if we work on ourselves, we make a fortune. If we remain stuck at one place that would be the death knell. Only those who keep evolving are able to harness their full potential. It is like termites eating away our talent, knowledge and understanding. Consistency leads to mediocrity. It is our inner demon squashing our talents which goes awry if not harnessed. A highly evolved and intelligent person will throw gauntlets at himself to grow. Anything that is stagnant is bound to decay. Many people have firm faith in consistency which is in fact a dangerous foe of growth. It leads to mental and physical inertia. We need to dabble in many myriad ways to do the same thing in a different way.

50

<u>Accepting challenges and risking failures make us formidable.</u>

If we take on the Goliath of challenges, we become intrepid. – Murli Chari

Even a trivial challenge puts many of us on the defensive and we give it up without a fight. Gauntlets are the ways of the universe to test us before rewarding abundantly. There is a very apt adage "We are not limited by challenges but we challenge the limits". This adage raises the glass ceiling to the ultimate. If we are inspired by this great saying we will transcend all the limits. There are many glaring examples of people swimming upstream. Dr. Helen Keller who was blind, deaf and dumb accomplished great things and was a great trend-setter. Many people took the challenges by their horns and broke all the records. Human lives are replete with people who achieved the impossible as they were daredevils. Human history is replete with examples of people challenging the odds to reach the apogee of achievements. Our own Sudha

Supreme Joy

Chandran despite having a broken leg with the help of legendary Jaipur foot gave a dance program. That gives ample evidence of what self-confidence and immense gumption can do to our ability to scale the Mount Everest of challenges. She acted in the Hindi film "Naache Mayuri" based on her own life. The legendary music director Late Ravindra Jain was a legendary music director and lyricist. The most incredible young Australian Nick Vujicic despite having no arms and legs literally does everything a normal human being is capable of doing. The legendary author Jim Stoval despite being blind is an ace swimmer, driver and pilot. His book The Ultimate Gifts is phenomenal. Those who accept challenges and takes responsible risks can do wonders. All afflictions are psychological. In spite of many afflictions some people are determined to do the best and make a niche position for themselves. If we treat challenges as an opportunity then we can do literally everything. Sheer determination can create miracles. When we treat challenges with reverence then the universe brings our desired dreams into reality. Challenges are a ploy by nature to bring out the best from us. Thomson Edison embraced challenges and turned out to be a legendary scientist. He has the most number of patents registered by any human being. By inventing the electric bulb Edison revolutionized the world. The bold and courageous turn challenges and failures into grand success. Dr. Martin Luther King Jr. took on the mighty whites and delivered the blacks from many scourges. There are many instances of people taking on the insurmountable challenges and creating history. Dr. Nelson Mandela accepted the gauntlet to dismantle the apartheid system. He was incarcerated in Robbin Islands in solitary cell. No personal discomfiture could dissuade this phenomenal warrior.

51

Rock the status quo

Those who remain in the rut are destined to be ruined. – Murli Chari

Majority of us go along with the trusted traditions as we lack courage to rock the status quo. Rocking the status quo is like swimming against the stream. Only the mediocre want to maintain the status quo as they are scared of leaving the comfort zone. Those who have vested interests favor the status quo. Plutocrats want the status quo so that they can continue to enjoy their wealth and power. Dr. George Bernard Shaw aptly quoted: The reasonable man adapts himself to the world; the unreasonable one persists in trying to adapt the world to himself. Therefore, all progress depends on the unreasonable man. Most of us are zombies scared to the bone to foray into the unknown terrain. Whatever progress we see in the world are by persons who are intrepid. Many of them risk their lives to make a paradigm shift. Galileo risked his life to challenge the traditional and biblical knowledge that all planets orbit around earth. Socrates had to consume hemlock and die for speaking the truth. Humans are hardwired to remain lazy. It takes immense gumption to challenge the status quo. At times one is required to risk his/her lives. Children are conditioned and brainstormed to take the beaten path. Only mavericks have the courage to challenge the status quo. We need grit, determination and phenomenal courage to challenge the status quo which is the exclusive preserve of the zombies.

We need to wake the people who are in deep comatose.

52

Mind is a monster if let loose

Unless we keep the mind in leash it will run berserk. – Murli Chari

Most of the human problems emanate from unruly minds. Mind can be our best ally or foe depending on how we use it. Mind is a social construct playing havoc in the world. Mind is the best servant and a bad master. Our minds are always busy judging, comparing, blaming, fretting, and criticizing. No doubt, human mind has invented oodles of things making human existence easy and comfortable. Minds are

Supreme Joy

vulnerable to be manipulated and indoctrinated. An untrammeled freedom to our minds will play havoc with the world. Adolf Hitler, Joseph Stalin, Mussolini and legions of others were slaves to their demonic minds. Our minds create chasms, walls and categorization based on religion, ideology, nation, caste, creed, race and gender. Once the mind goes berserk, we are powerless and become victims of the machinations of our own minds. We need to time and again remove the gibberish that get accumulated in our minds. Physical scars may get healed over a period of time but the psychological scars remain ensconced in our minds. Human mind, no doubt, has created many marvels making our lives enjoyable and comfortable. Ironically mind has created weapons of mass destruction, spoilt the ecological balance, plundered the planet, polluted the rivers, oceans, atmosphere, marauded the nature, sent many species to extinction and caused untold devastation. Mind needs immense support from intuition, emotions, instinct, awareness, consciousness imagination, intellect, intelligence and creativity. Unfortunately, we rely more on our minds which is ego-centric. The most wonderful gift of the universe is the sub-conscious mind which is a storehouse of many experiences and runs the human body mechanism. Even while we are in deep sleep the subconscious continues to pump blood, breathe and do myriads of things without our conscious effort. However, modern man relies heavily on rational mind. Our subconscious mind stores all the events which we tend to forget. Our rational mind has done irreparable loss to the mother nature which has endowed us with a cornucopia of affluence. Mind which is very ego-centric, ruthless, avaricious, insensitive and demonic has played havoc with the world. Mind creates all the hubris, genocides and avarice.

53

Find a way or fade away.

We can wriggle out of any imbroglio if we are determined. – Murli Chari

Most of us give up at the first sight of a problem. That is the reason why millions fail to succeed. In fact, our universe sends problems on our way to strengthen us. Millions upon millions get stuck in the rut and do not try alternatives. They resign to their fates. The eternal wisdom "Where there is will there is a way" comes to our aid when we encounter problems. When we face a problem if we understand the anatomy of the problem half our problem is solved. We can always take the help of experts in the field who can help us to resolve the problem. When we solve a problem, we grow in stature and strength. If we fail to find a way we will fade away. We need to learn from the giants who found a way out of the most intractable issues. There are many glaring examples of greats who took the problems by the horns and came out victorious. We can as well seek the help of those who faced similar problems and vanquished them. Necessity is the mother of invention is an oft-repeated proverb which has served many people who were beset by the problems. Cure for many illnesses is a classic example of finding a way or fade away.

54

<u>Kindness is free and contagious. Price: 0</u>

Kindness is love in action. Surprisingly kindness is free and contagious is free as well. This virtue can make us divine self. Kindness can do wonders and practiced by all our world would certainly become a paradise. It is sublime compassion. With kindness we can tame the wild animals and brutes in the form of human beings. Kindness is one of the best virtues we human beings can possess. We may have seen how showing kindness invokes love in human beings and all sentient beings. Kindness creates magic. Kindness permeates through our whole being. A rampant elephant gone berserk charged towards Gautam Buddha but Buddha's kindness made the frenzied elephant fall prostrate on the feet of the great sage. Dalai Llama is one of the greatest practitioners of kindness. He forgives even those who had malice towards him. Kindness transcends all negative feelings like envy, anger, hatred and violence. It requires phenomenal courage, humility, empathy and love. One who is kind will have legions of friends. It is a great fountainhead of love. Kindness is the elixir of life.

55

<u>Purpose of life is a life of purpose</u>

To wander aimlessly serves no purpose and is an insult to the benevolent universe. – Murli Chari

Purpose is much deeper and more subtle that goals and objectives look minnows. Goals make us anxious and create stress. On the other hand, purpose leads to inspired and cheerful action. Purpose makes us get up in the morning. It is all encompassing as it has enthusiasm and empathy for all. Purpose in life is a perennial source of exuberance, bliss and joy. Goals on the other hand, lead to selfishness, and make us braggadocios and grumpy. They make us hedonist and Narcissists. Purpose makes us humble and goals make us arrogant and haughty. Whilst pursuing goals we become melancholy and saturnine. On the other hand, being on purpose leads to ecstasy, euphoria and exhilaration. Goals make us a social recluse. We may get all the worldly riches but lose our conscience. When we have no qualms of conscience then we are prone to committing treacherous things. We have legions of examples in human history on how Adolf Hitler, Mussolini, Idi Amin, Joseph Stalin et al pursuing their individual goals committed genocide killing and maiming millions. On the other hand, people like Dr. Martin Luther King, Jr., Mahatma Gandhi lived and acted for a purpose larger than their individual lives. All the carnage, devastation, mayhem and bloodshed are due to people pursuing their goals which benefit themselves only. Pursuit of goals make us cantankerous, dull and drab. Purpose keeps us lively and exhilarating. If each one of us resorts to purpose rather than goals the world would be a wonderful place. Goals usually pit us against others. There are fraying of tempers and throw of tantrums. Goals make us a serious player without enjoying the game. On the other hand, purpose keeps us enthusiastic, cheerful and excited. Purpose serves the larger good. When on purpose we enjoy the journey as well rather than becoming dull and drab whilst pursuing goals. Purpose attracts the dimensions of a large swathe of people who cooperate as they also become beneficiaries. In goals most of the time they are self-serving. Goals lead to attrition of valuable resources and purpose leads to build up the momentum as it adds value to millions. Purpose leads to cooperation and goals to competition. Millions are in the Cul-de- sac jobs going through the motions doing mundane and routine jobs. They do not put their heart and soul into their jobs. This serves no purpose. Having a purpose brings out the magic within us.

It's time we all did soul-searching and finding our true purpose. Each one of us is endowed with immense treasure trove of talents which can be explored and exploited if one has a compelling purpose. To understand the anatomy of purpose please read Ikigai which is a Japanese term for purpose. Purpose creates alignment between our thoughts, speech and action. There is no dichotomy. Such a situation creates phenomenal cosmic energy and limitless energy to carry out what we think of. Think of the purpose of founding fathers of United States of America. They were chosen ten committed patriots who signed a memorandum to seek freedom for their country from Great Britain. That is a classic case of purpose. Goals consider sectarian view as against wide gamut of purpose. The inimitable, indubitable and bold leader Dr. Nelson Mandela who was in incarceration in the solitary jail in Robbin Islands for 27 years had the sole purpose to dismantle apartheid. The success ratio of those who have purposes are far more than those who have goals. Purpose is our own goals aligned with the larger community. It benefits many. On the other hand, goals make us self-centered, self-focused and cantankerous. Purpose releases all positive enzymes like dopamine, serotonin and endocrines. You are elevated to the levels of divinity. Goals make you feel hubris, in competition with others and cornered. Goals release negative enzymes like cortisol and adrenal. Now that we have lot of clarity about purposes and goals it is very clear that we all need to embrace purpose over goals. Goals create malice, ill health and stress. Purpose on the other hand is elixir for life and longevity. Goals are mostly left-brained activity which fails to make use of the right-brained activity like intuition, imagination, awareness, instinct, and creativity.

56

We need to rid ourselves of all illusions.

The greatest wisdom is all that we experience and think are illusions. – Murli Chari

Human lives are full of illusions. We human beings are prone to accepting obsolete beliefs from our well-meaning parents, friends, relatives, religious and political leaders, teachers, ideologies, governments and media. If we fail to call the bluffs and shenanigans of politicians, we would surrender to the illusions created by these charlatans. Every belief, every idea, every faith, and every ideology are some sort of illusion. Illusions are like mirages in the desert leading us nowhere. Most of the beliefs, religious tenets, ideologies and faith may be innocuous or a veiled trap. As far as scientific beliefs are concerned, they are genuine and authentic as the findings are universally testable. Sacrifices, obligations and discipline most of the times are a ploy and mostly illusory to serve those who are fishing in troubled waters. For eons superstitious beliefs are considered authentic and unchallengeable. Our world is illusions galore. When we are under the spell of illusions, we perceive a rope as a snake and a snake as a rope. When we are under the magic spell of illusions our rational minds are paralyzed. We need to besmirch most of the illusions which have been accepted without checking its credibility to live a blissful life. We need to be intrepid to challenge the illusions. It is always better to fully understand and then have conviction rather than blindly following the beliefs. Most of the beliefs we take for granted are the reasons for our misery. Even our perceptions, assumptions, faiths, beliefs and understanding are flawed as they have not been thoroughly scrutinized. Illusions create havoc and lead to genocide and most of the violences in the world. When we are inebriated with a certain belief system, we go to any extent to defend it. All the animosity in the world can be traced to distorted belief systems. Illusions make us parochial and paranoid. The Indian mythology calls everything Maya meaning illusion. So, let's be free from illusions to enjoy supreme joy and bliss. Our lives are meant to be fun and joy.

57

We need to make the most of all resources available to us.

The secret to success is to fully exploit all the resources at hand. – Murli Chari

Each one of us is endowed with far more resources than we can make use of. There is unlimited supply of resources ensuring abounding affluence for all and sundry. Poverty has been there due to faulty and skewed thinking. Each one of us can be as rich as Elon Musk or Jeff Bezos. The greatest asset in the world is knowledge and wisdom. It's not equities businesses, real estates, gold, platinum, diamond and money but a sound idea. Shares may give a return of say 40% per annum, knowledge may give more than one billion times. We need to leverage all the resources. To get a good idea it is recommended that you read all the books by Robert Kiyosaki. To name a few they are Rich Dad Poor Dad, Retire Young Retire Rich, Business School and Cash Quadrant. We need to first set our dreams that we would love to achieve. Its time the governments across the globe improved the quality of human beings rather than focusing on building high quality infrastructure. Once we fully utilize all the resources in our sprawling universe we would improve the lives of billions. That way we can forever besmirch the skewed philosophy that making money is a cardinal sin. Most of the religions propagate this ideology. There is an internecine war going on in our minds about which philosophy to follow. We need to embrace the philosophy of abundance as we can easily understand the humongous universe. If the creator wanted us to live in penury, he would not have created the wonderful extravaganza of abundance in the universe. Human beings have totally been oblivious to this reality.

I am immensely grateful to the readers for spending their time, money and effort to buy and read the book. My vision is to create happy one billion billionaires across the globe. You may visit my website www.murlichari.in to have access to all my blogs, podcasts, videos, vision and mission. I am sanguine that all the human beings will benefit by reading this book as well as going through my contents on my website.

Warm Regards

Murli Chari

Supreme Joy

Supreme Joy

Supreme Joy

www.ingramcontent.com/pod-product-compliance
Lightning Source LLC
Chambersburg PA
CBHW041336120726
48005CB00014B/2281